Queen of the Kisses

By Sheryl Wolff Kayne

To my parents, Nat and Ruth Wolff, and my children, Ellie and Aviva Kayne, who share the magic in their own special way.

Text copyright @ 1994 by Sheryl Wolff Kayne.
Illustrations copyright @ 1994 by Meribeth Blonski.
All rights Reserved including the right of reproduction
in whole or in part in any form.

Library of Congress Catalog # 94-75985

Library of Congress Cataloging in Publication Data
Kayne, Sheryl Wolff
Queen of the Kisses

Summary: A tale of Queen Theresa, also known
at Queen of Kisses, and how she
solves a little girl's problem of dried-up kisses

1. Children's Stories, American. [1. Kiss-Fiction]
1. Blonski, Meribeth, ill   11. Title

Printed in Hong Kong
ISBN# 1-880851-13-X

Published by:
Greene Bark Press Inc.,
PO Box 1108
Bridgeport, CT 06601-1108

Queen Theresa waves her wand left and right
as the Kissing Helper trainees recite their pledge:
"Give a kiss today. Get a kiss today. Share the
magic in your own special way."

"Beautiful! Give each other your best good morning kiss and we will begin our lesson," says Queen Theresa as she kisses each of her students. "Who remembers what we learned yesterday? Jenny?"

2

"Everyone is born knowing how to kiss!"
"We all need to kiss and be kissed everyday,"
adds Michael.

"Yes," says Donna Rae, "and too often, people save kissing for special occasions. Kisses are for all of the time!"

6

"What a wonderful class! You were all listening and learning. Today's lesson is about magic kisses. When we least expect it, and most need it, and think there are no kisses left in the whole wide world for us," Queen Theresa stops talking as the Emergency Kissing Siren suddenly begins to howl: "Help Kiss! Help Kiss!" Prince Marty runs right into the middle of the class.

"Queen Theresa, Queen Theresa! We have an emergency and no one knows what to do! A little girl woke up this morning and says her kisses have all dried up! She doesn't have any kisses left! They've just disappeared."

"Oh, my! Princess Marguerite and Prince Alabaster specialize in problem cases."

"But Queen Theresa, Princess Marguerite is in Alaska working with Eskimos' noses and Prince Alabaster is on vacation in Miami Beach," says Prince Marty, shaking his head. "What shall we do?"

Queen Theresa takes a deep breath, "I'm teaching and can't leave my class. Plus, I haven't handled an emergency in many years. There must be someone else who can help. What about you, Prince Marty?"

"I volunteered to go," says Prince Marty, "but I don't know how to fly the Kissmobile. This little girl lives in New York City. That is much too far to fly on wing power alone."

8

"Dried up kisses are very unusual," says Queen Theresa, remembering hearing her mother, Queen Momma, talk about them. "I've worked with forgotten kisses, sad kisses, happy kisses, hello kisses, goodbye kisses, but never dried up kisses." Queen Theresa turns around and closes her eyes.

Help is needed in a hurry. She can't say no. She looks at the Kissing Helper trainees. "Prince Marty, please teach my class while I prepare the Kissmobile." The helpers clap and cheer.

Before take-off, Queen Theresa checks the supply of flying kisses, pucker dust, kissing potions numbers one, two, three and four, and the emergency kit she has never needed before, but this is a very unusual case.

"Dried up kisses," she mumbles to herself, throwing handfuls of flying kisses into the air to start the Kissmobile. "I'll try everything I know."

The sky is clear and bright. She sets the Kiss
panels on New York City and begins making her
plans. The Kiss Radar hiccups, "Trouble ahead!"
It takes almost the full supply of flying kisses to
get up and over The World Trade Center.

Queen Theresa sighs with relief as she nears East
57th Street. "Oh, dear, where will I park?" Emptying
a bag of flying kisses to get high enough to park on the
roof, the Kissmobile lands quietly in a vegetable garden,
with a sand box on the left and a tennis court on the right.

13

Queen Theresa flutters by the windows, looking for an open one on the ninth floor. No luck. Her wings are rustier than she thought. She makes a mental note to practice flying with the Kissing Helper trainess as soon as she gets back.

"Now what is that?" Queen Theresa pauses to listen at one lone open window. A sad voice drifts out to her, "Mommy, I don't know where they went."

14

"So, this is the little girl," hums Queen Theresa.

A girl is sitting at the breakfast table, crying into her cereal. Puddles of tears splash onto the tablecloth and floor. "All of my kisses have dried up. I don't have one left for you or Daddy or even Bare Bear."

"Emily," says Mommy, "let me give you just one little peck on the cheek." She leans over, but Emily jumps to her feet yelling, "No! No! No kisses at all!" Emily runs to her room and flops down on her bed.

Queen Theresa follows. She stands on the bed post, pucker
dust ready. First she sprinkles a pinch above Emily's head on the
pillow. Nothing. Not even a wink. Then she pours a whole
handful on Emily's mouth. Well, Emily just licks it off with her
tongue and goes to sleep.

"Oh, my, what next?" says Queen Theresa. She sees a bucket
in the toy pile, fills it with pucker dust, shovels it onto Emily's eyes,
ears, nose, lips, chin, cheeks, fingers and toes. Emily's lips begin
to pucker, her eyes open with a twinkle and she puts her fingers
on her lips before turning over and going back to sleep.

Queen Theresa takes out her kissing potions. They always work, but first Emily has to wake up! Queen Theresa flies around Emily's bed, lightly kissing her. Emily sits up and tries to kiss Bare Bear, but can't, making her cry again.

"Oh, my, this isn't good," mumbles the Queen. She squirts the potions directly at Emily, the first, the second, the third and the fourth. Emily stops crying. Emily manages to smile, but she doesn't pucker, not even a little bit.

Queen Theresa has no choice, she definitely needs the Emergency Kit Queen Momma gave her when she retired, "To be used only in a true emergency, Theresa. Try everything else first!"

The grey metal box squeaks open and Emily jumps up, looking around her room. The squeak turns into a buzz. The Kissing Bug is free at last.

The Kissing Bug aims for the window. "No, little Kissing Bug, before you fly away, Emily needs your help or she may never be able to kiss again."

Kissing Bug turns to lean on her wing, "My name is Gladys, if you please. If I bug that little girl, do you promise to let me go free?"

"Yes, Gladys, I do."

Gladys straightens her wings, stretches out her antennae, and takes aim. Flying off, Gladys bugs Emily on the right cheek, then the left, the forehead and smack dab in the middle of her rounded chin. Gladys winds up her stinger to give Emily the final zinger —squarely on the lips.

Sure her job is done, Gladys leaves to buzz around New York City as Queen Theresa gently moves Emily into the living room near her mother to see all of the new kisses which will be coming out any minute. "Hi, Emily, do you feel better now?"

"Yes, I feel much better. I had a nap."

"May I kiss you like I always do when you wake up?"

21

"No, Mommy, I told you, I don't have any kisses left! They are all dried up!" says Emily.

Queen Theresa cannot believe it. She lies down on the floor, kicking and screaming and kissing and kissing! "I can't go back to my class until all of this business is finished," she cries. The pucker dust, kissing potions and even Gladys didn't work.

Queen Theresa picks herself up, "What to do? What to do?" She shakes her head and then it comes to her, "The magic kiss, the magic kiss," she remembers from the lesson she prepared to give to her class. "When we least expect it, and most need it, and think there are no kisses left in the whole wide world for us, we each have our own special magic kiss waiting deep down inside. Close your eyes, stay very still and quiet while you let your magic grow. Pucker up and feel the magic."

Queen Theresa reaches way down inside to feel her magic, waits patiently while it tingles up, puckers her biggest pucker, and ever ,so gently flies straight at Emily's mouth, "Smack!" and flies straight to Emily's mother's mouth, "Smack!"

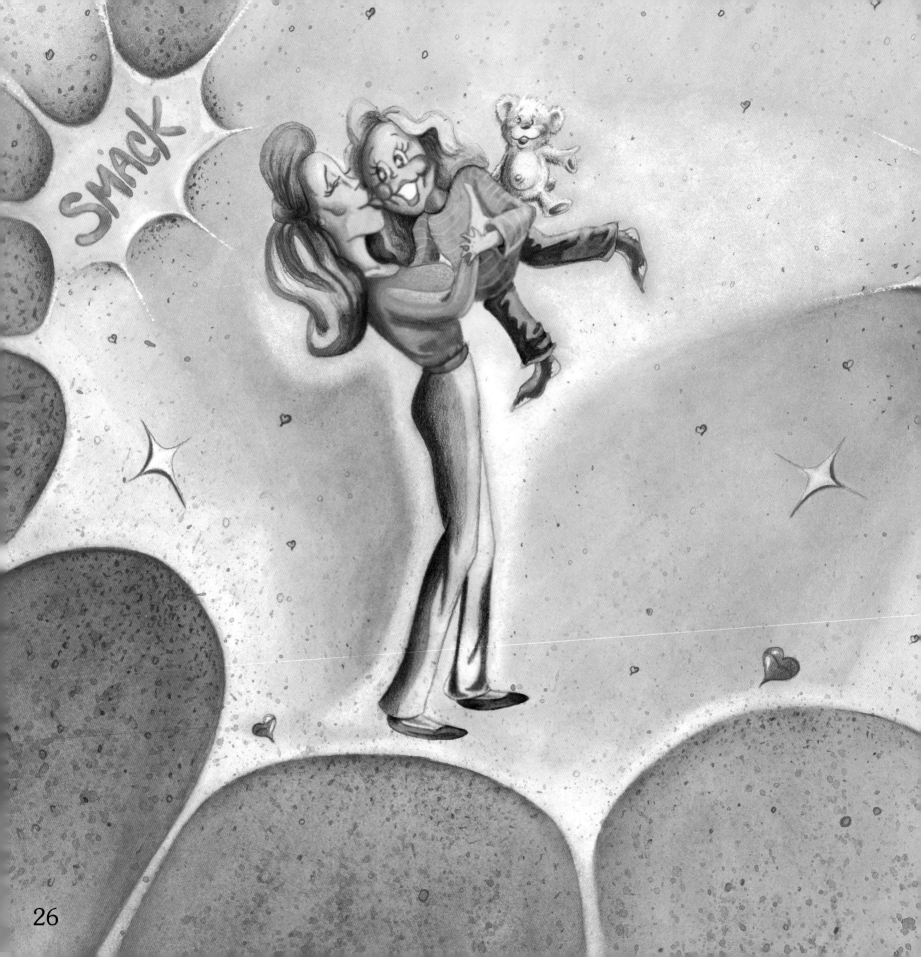

26

Suddenly she hears, "Smack! Mmmwah! Smooch!"
Emily can't stop kissing. Her mother can't stop kissing.
Even Bare Bear can't stop kissing.

27

Queen Theresa quietly bows out through the window
and heads for her Kissmobile and turns on the Kissadio.

28

"Prince Marty, kisses restored. I had the magic kiss with me all of the time," she laughs.

"Tell my class I'm on my way home to share the magic.
Kissy, kissy and out."